We're Very Good Friends, My Brother and I

Written and illustrated

by

P. K. Hallinan

For my sons, Ken and Mike,
whose brotherly love
inspired this book.

Ideals Children's Books • Nashville, Tennessee
an imprint of Hambleton-Hill Publishing, Inc.

Published by Ideals Children's Books
An imprint of Hambleton-Hill Publishing, Inc.
Nashville, Tennessee 37218

Printed and bound in the United States of America

ISBN 0-8249-8469-2

We're very good friends,
my brother and I.

We go for long walks;

we watch clouds go by.

And sometimes we just don't
see eye to eye—
but that's okay,
we're friends anyway.

We laugh a lot, too,
my brother and I.

We like to run fast

and pretend we can fly.

And sometimes we'll lie
in a pile of sand
and talk about places
in faraway lands.

Or sometimes we'll stand
and not talk at all—
but that's okay, too,
we're friends, after all.

We do lots of fun things,
my brother and I.

We hop all around;

we fall on the ground.

We hide in the forest
when a monster's around.

And sometimes we'll swing
on the branch of a tree,

or sit in a puddle
and pretend it's the sea.

And sometimes we'll stare
at a bird in the air
and stand so still that
we don't move a hair . . .

which isn't easy
when the wind is breezy.

And sometimes at night,
we'll turn off the light
and act very creepy
until we get sleepy
or someone gets scared.

We act creepy a lot,
my brother and I.

But mostly we like
to play out of doors,

17

or look at our books,

or help out with chores.

And once in awhile
we'll play on our own—
but it isn't much fun—
and when all's said and done . . .

being together
beats being alone.

So even when we're mad
or just feeling sad,

we're still always glad
to be brothers.

And I guess in the end
that's the best reason why

we're very good friends,
my brother and I!